Free teaching resources!

Scan the QR code (or follow the link) to access free printable teaching resources. Purple Mash subscribers* can access additional interactive online resources! Just search KOBE inside Purple Mash.

www.purplemashpublishing.com/pages/kobe

*You can start a free trial of Purple Mash by visiting www.2simple.com

Kobe Ketchup and the Food Bank Adventure

By Madelaine Black

Illustrated by Shirley Waisman

Published in the UK by Purple Mash Publishing an imprint of 2 Simple Publishing Ltd
5 Broadbent Close, London, United Kingdom, N6 5JW
Company number 08608270

This book has been published in support of Bankuet Ltd
Company number 11903616

Bankuet will receive £1.05 from every book sale,
of which £1 will be donated to food banks

ISBN 978-1-7398251-3-3

Printed in the UK by Pollards

www.purplemashpublishing.com

In support of

Bankuet

Hey! Is ketchup your favourite sauce?
To have with other things, of course!

But imagine you didn't have anything else
to eat with the ketchup that sits on your shelf.

3

Our story begins with a boy named Jay
who made his own lunch for school every day.
He always looked forward to sandwich and treat,
and the ring of the bell that meant TIME TO EAT!

Today Mum spoke with tears in her eyes.
"Jay, things aren't good, I won't tell you lies.
I've got no work. Nothing's left in my purse.
No money for food. It couldn't get worse."

He was used to there being less food around.
But still Jay's tummy made a rumbling sound.
Yet, he said to himself, "I will not complain,
there's only ketchup for my sandwich, again!"

Today was Ms Mistry's turn on lunch duty.
She watched as her class unpacked their lunch booty.
She noticed Jay sitting alone by the tree,
opening his lunch box so no one could see.

Lenny had tuna. Benny had ham.
Julie had cheese, and Priti had jam.
Their lunch boxes bulged with chocolates and snacks,
and yoghurts and crackers, and crisps in bright packs.

Inside Jay's lunch box was nothing so nice.
Just a squirt of ketchup on one folded slice.
Ms Mistry went over to where he was sat.
"Hello there, Jay. Can we have a quick chat?"

Ms Mistry asked him how things were at home.
With someone to talk to Jay felt less alone.
He told her how he and Mum used to have plenty,
But now Mum's purse and cupboard were empty.

She gave him a voucher to take to his mum.
"You swap this for food that will fill up your tum.
You can get what you need at the food bank.
Such a welcoming place run by my friend Frank!"

8

Back home Jay said, "Mum, there's nothing to eat.
Let's go to the food bank just down our street!
Mrs Freeman was there to get food and support.
I helped with her bags when I got home from sport."

"No, we won't be going," Mum snapped in a mood,
"Mrs Freeman must need it much more than we do.
I won't ask for help. I'm sure we'll be fine.
I'm embarrassed to go there and wait in that line!"

Jay searched in the cupboard for something for tea.
Two half empty bottles were all he could see.
Some lonely red ketchup and white mayonnaise,
And nothing else sitting beside them for days!

Then the cupboard lit up with a bright magic glow.
OFF TO THE FOOD BANK! COME ON. LET'S GO!

The mayo and ketchup had come alive.
"Red sauce to the rescue! I'm Kobe. High five!
Meet Nao the Mayo and her Little Sachets.
We're all at your service. Up, up, and away!

With Kobe and Nao, fish fingers taste great!
We go well with chips and the rice on your plate.
Together with you we'll come up with a plan.
There's no reason for you to go hungry young man."

"Great," said Jay, "how 'bout this Saturday?
Our football team has a big game to play.
I'll put on my kit, and pick up my ball,
and tell Mum the team meet is up at the hall."

"Ace!" Kobe said, "Mum will have you to thank
when you've got your supplies from that friendly food bank."
"Wow!" Nao cheered. "What a fine proposition!
Me and my Sachets are on for this mission!"

14

The day of the Food Bank Adventure arrived.
Frank had been in there since half-past five.
Ms Mistry sent him this message to say:
Young Jay will come in with his mum today.

Jay opened the door for his Mum to enter.
Frank greeted them warmly "Welcome to our Centre!
It's where local people can gather and share.
Not enough food at home? We're here to care."

"Please come inside for a cuppa and chat.
Things will get better, we're sure of that.
You can stock yourself up for the next few days.
We're ready to help you in all kinds of ways."

"You'll find boxes and packets, baskets and cans.
Food comes here in crates which we sort by hand.
Some of the people you see working here
Are the folk who so generously volunteer."

18

Kobe and Nao were along for the ride.
Jay opened his bag, and Mum looked inside.
"Meet my friends, Mum. We're on an adventure."
The Little Sachets bounced out over the Centre.

Mum stared in shock, her mouth hung agape.
"Talking sauces? Ketchup dressed in a cape?!
I am glad we are here, though I was afraid
Somebody might see us asking for aid."

They gave Frank the voucher. He took it and smiled.
"Young Jay is so helpful. A wonderful child!
What food can we give you – you and your boy –
to take home together, to cook and enjoy?

There's tuna, there's pasta. There's oil, there's rice.
Some salt and some pepper. Some sugar and spice.
Flour for pancakes. Potatoes to fry.
Lots of good things to help you get by."

There was still time for football, so no need to hurry.
After talking with Frank, Mum let go of her worry.
Jay put on an apron to sort the donations
"You're part of the team Jay. Congratulations!"

Jay and his mum walked home hand in hand.
They had food in their bags, just as Jay had planned.
It no longer mattered that someone might see them.
Then who should they meet in the street? Mrs Freeman!

Mrs Freeman called out, "Did your team win today?
Please help me carry my bags again Jay.
I've got something to give you – this chocolate bar!
A small little gift to help me say 'ta'!"

At suppertime Jay and his mum felt relieved.
They unpacked the yummy food they'd received.
They cooked tasty pasta covered in sauce,
And added the ketchup and mayo, of course!

They chopped up carrots, grated cheese with the grater.
They snacked as they cooked; they could not wait till later!
"That food bank's a blessing," Mum kissed Jay on the cheek.
"It's so good to know we could go there next week."

26

Delicious smells from their kitchen filled up the air.
Pasta with peas, beans and carrots to share.

But before they sat down, Kobe jumped to exclaim,

"Now, here is something I want to explain!

It takes all of us: sorters and packers
Clients or helpers, it just doesn't matter
Together. Connected. We all are agreed:
Our community's here to help people in need."

27

28

Mission accomplished, our heroes felt great.
They squirted and squiggled all over each plate.
Even Mum didn't fuss about making a mess
As they splashed on Jay's T-shirt, and splished on her dress.

30

And now here's a message from the Food Bank,
Is there a volunteer to read it? "I will" says Frank!

You may have neighbours right here on your street,
with not enough food for their families to eat.
We must all understand that it's just not OK
for anyone to have to live in this way.

We each have special powers to make our world fair,
like Kindness and Caring and Learning to Share.
Let's help one another and together make sure
One day we won't need food banks anymore!

31

About the Author
Madelaine Black
www.madelaineblack.com

Madelaine Black's favourite thing to do is share funny stories and silly songs with her grandchildren. Her other favourite thing to do is to help charities and non-profits to raise funds and awareness.

She has spent 35 years as an award-winning creative consultant, and she calls what she does "creativit that matters".

The idea for this book about a magical talking ketchup bottle popped into Madelaine's head after an inspiring morning she spent volunteering at her local food bank.

About the Illustrator
Shirley Waisman
www.shirleywaisman.com

Shirley Waisman has been drawing and painting as long as she can remember, and has illustrated more than 50 books for children. Her greatest reward is seeing children smiling as they enjoy her illustrations.

She studied her craft in Israel and Japan. Shirley Waisman is a graduate of the Bezalel Academy of Arts and Design with a BA in visual communication. She was awarded a research scholarship that allowed her to spend two years in Japan researching children's book illustration.

Today, she works as an illustrator while also working on her Master's degree in art and education.

Bankuet

Bankuet is the UK's first digital zero-waste food donation platform and the number one supplier of food to food banks.

A business for good, our mission is to provide food banks with what they need, when they need it – and to make it easier for donors to give and continue to tackle the food poverty problem that currently exists in the UK.

The innovative model enables funds raised by the click of a button via the platform to bulk purchase essential items that food banks have requested in advance, from our trusted food retailers. The efficient model ensures zero-waste, preventing surplus by identifying and delivering exactly what is needed.

For every copy of this book sold, £1 goes to a food bank in the Bankuet network.

You can learn more about how Bankuet is helping food banks on our website.

www.bankuet.co.uk

*In 2021 Bankuet were named
Economic Innovator of the Year for London and the South-East
at The Spectator Economic Innovators Awards.*

Other titles you might enjoy

All of the books below can be purchased from
www.purplemashpublishing.com or www.amazon.co.uk

Striker Boy
Written by Jonny Zucker
£6.99 | Published in aid of Mind

Nat Dixon is Premier League Football Club Hatton Rangers' mystery new signing – and their only chance of avoiding relegation. It's every young footballer's dream come true and Nat feels as though he's fulfilling his destiny... But what his fellow players, the fans and the press don't know is that Nat is only 13 years old...

REDCAP
Written by June Mari Louise Lipka, illustrated by Ginger Gilmour
£7.99 | Published in aid of ActionAid

This is an inspiring and uplifting story about a little boy called REDCAP, who lives with his MOTHER in the enchanted WILDWOOD. He is such a happy fellow and all the creatures in the forest love him. One day his mum becomes ill and he is determined to look after her and make her well.

Going to the Fair & other poems
Written by Sue Gordon, illustrated by Hâf Gardner
£3.99 | Published in aid of Noah's Ark Children's Hospice

A charming collection of playful poems by Sue Gordon, beautifully illustrated by Hâf Gardner. Sue's poems and Hâf's illustrations are sure to amuse, delight and excite children.